Bed of Rejection

Secret Lies

By Stephanie M. Captain

Dedication

Jesus, this one is for you and you alone. I love you.

1

I tip toed into the house and quietly placed my purse on the table in the foyer. I did not hear the chime for the security system. I figured it was off for some odd reason; however, in the moment, I could not think of what the reason could be. It was 6:30 in the evening, and my little stop to see the Christmas lights and listen to the carolers had me way past my curfew. I knew I couldn't say I had worked late because he would look for the extra time on my next pay check. It was in my thinking of an excuse to appease my husband that the first blow came. The blow to my back took my breath away and knocked me to the floor. I knew better than to scream. That meant the beating would be more severe.

"Where have you been you little black whore?"

He had been drinking. I could smell it in the rushed words that hatred forced from his mouth. The rage in his voice made my heart tremble. He knew I would not cheat on him. Ever. That was his character and he did not care that I knew about her. All he wanted was an excuse. Any excuse to bring me to the brink of death as often as he felt like it. I did not matter to him.

"Answer me!"

Jerking me from the marble floor he twist my arm behind my back to the point that I was certain it would pop off like the little plastic doll's arms I played with as I child. I tried to hurriedly think of an excuse. I dared not tell him I was gazing at the Christmas lights, listening to the carolers, and regretting my choices in life. He did not believe in God and that would only prolong the beating. Through my labored breathing I answered him as he had demanded. "Traffic was bad. There was an accident."

The moment I said it I regretted not thinking fast enough. He would know if there was an accident. Somehow he always knew everything that took place in my life; no matter where I went or what I did.

"Liar!" The blow and the word, both filled with venom found me at the same time. Because he still held my arm behind my back, I could not shield myself from him kneeing me in my private area. I felt like all of my insides would fall to the ground. I had not been able to stifle the scream that flew from my mouth in response to my 280 pound, 6'3" husband using me as a punching bag. My pain amused him and for the first time after being taught a lesson, he let me go hastily.

"Tonight you are preparing dinner for one; me. I expect for my steak to be medium well, the brown rice to be perfect and not mushy, and my asparagus crisp. I want my apple cobbler warmed with a side of vanilla ice cream. You have one hour. Do I make myself clear?"

I do not cry. My pain button had been muted. All I needed to do was survive. My swollen arm that he had twisted behind my back still stirred the rice and kneaded the dough. Worrying about going to bed hungry was not on my list. My only concern was that I only had fifty-seven minutes. I constantly watched the clock. Knowing one minute past his deadline could cost me. While preparing his meal; my mind drifted back to my wedding day.

"But Mommy he is a good man."

"Why? Because he is white and has money? Does he love you? Will he take care of you if you stop making six figures? If you were not an attorney would he have even given you a second glance? Your father and I did not struggle to send you to school so you could marry the first man that came along as soon as you were finally stable enough to give back to us."

"Is that what this is about, money? I found someone who loves me for who I am. Mommy he does love me. I have never known a man like him. Why can't you just be happy for me?"

"It is hard to be happy when all I see is control. Why aren't any of your friends or relatives in the wedding? Why do you have to move to a gated community in which we must have permission to visit you? His permission. That is not love. You need to open your eyes little girl."

"No Mommy I am not a little girl. I am an adult and that is the problem. I am not your little baby anymore. You cannot make my decisions for me. You and Daddy are having a hard time accepting that."

"What we cannot accept is the fact that you are so in love that you have thrown all caution to the wind. When the right man comes along he does not eliminate your family; he embraces them. What you think is love is just jealousy that will soon turn into anger and rage."

"Are you serious Mommy? Because my soon to be husband wants to have a little time for us to be together as newlyweds you say he is an abuser. He has never treated me with anything but respect. He opens the door for me. He treats me like a lady. He ensures I only dress, drive and eat the finest. Is there something wrong with that? I am his queen."

Her mother's laugh sears her nerves, but not as much as her words.

"Queen? However could that be possible?"

Anger erupts. "You think a white man can't have a black queen? Mother, you are a racist. Love doesn't have boundaries mother, and I refuse to marry someone I do not love. I think it is sad that you and Daddy decided that happiness could only be found among your own kind. Well, I found it in mankind and that is enough for me. Finn and I will make it. Just wait and see."

The phone rings and she answers; leaving the room, her parents' home, and their life. The next day, as soon as she became Mrs. Finn Bardo, everything changed; her address, her phone number, her life.

The timer on the stove reminds me of my surroundings again. Placing the meal on the silver tray, I hurriedly make my way to the private study where my husband of eighteen months sat with his eyes closed. My cell phone is on his lap. I know he has gone through my contacts, calls, and texts. That did not matter. It had been a long time since anyone had called me and even longer since I had reached out to anyone. For just a few seconds, I longed for him to be the man I thought he had been. The one I needed him to be. The one I thought desperately loved me and had to have me as his wife. The man my mother had known all along he was not.

He kept a low haircut. It was the only way to manage the unruly black hair he hated so much. His light brown eyes, not noticeable at the present, gave life to his entire face. The humor, the twinkle, the warmth in them drew me to him that day in the post office where we had first met. The day seemed like it was forever times infinity. Having dropped off the mail from the company I worked for, Finn had immediately come to my rescue after a rude patron bumped into me causing it to fall to the ground. I reached down to retrieve my parcels and met his eyes. Alluring, daring, inviting eyes that were placed among strong distinct features. He was rugged, yet handsome enough to turn a few heads. As he did that day when he stopped to help a damsel in distress.

"Here is your food Finn. Just the way you like it."

"It had better be. You can run my bathwater after you clean the kitchen and iron my clothes for tomorrow."

"Is there anything else I can do for you Finn?"

That made him nervous and I knew it. I could not beat him at his game but I could make him wonder how I could be nice to him after he treated me with such distain. I was well aware that my punishment from him was starvation. Being sent to bed without dinner was something heartless parents did to their children. Yet my husband used the technique to try and get even with me each time I reminded him that he was married to a woman that he did not love. He ignored my question. That was answer enough.

As I cleaned the house I despised, and ironed clothing for a man who despised me, there was only one thing on my mind. Portland. My husband could not go with me there and for nine days I would have peace. For nine days no one would hit me, treat me like trash, and I would eat as much as I wanted using the company credit card. That was where my solace came, an unexpected business trip to work long hours with a workaholic boss who lived and breathed his job.

2

Driving away from my six bedroom home in Wilson Heights in Atlanta the next morning, I smiled. My somber husband stood watching from the window. No goodbye. No good luck. Just anger. Anger that was a result of him not being able to control my job situation. The one that allowed me to be away from his fist and his tyranny for just a little while. While away, I could try to reconcile things with my parents, catch up with my friends, and to make decisions and choices that did not include him. Away. It was all I could think of.

Before leaving I actually considered going into the bedroom that used to be ours to see my husband. Not sure why, but I just wanted to so badly. My heart cried for him. For what should have been. A part of me thought of the reasons I fell so madly in love with him. Why I had to have him. Thought of him so much in the beginning. Had to hear his voice. A very small part of me needed to hope that perhaps we could salvage our marriage. I needed to see him, the one that used to call me on the phone just to hear my voice. Tickle me just so he could hear my laugh. Take pictures of me so he could look through them when he missed me during the day. The romantic in me fantasized about him being sorry. Telling me he loved me. Holding me, and begging me to stay with him. Him telling me that he not only wanted me, but he desperately needed me in his life. I imagined he would say we could start over again and make our marriage work. That we could start a family in a couple of years. I actually wanted to apologize for whatever I had done to make him hate me so. When he thrust out of the bedroom door and walked past me without so much as looking my way, I knew it was pointless. To him I was nonexistent.

Having to run by the office to pick up the itinerary I'd forgotten, I could not resist the urge to call my parents again from my office phone. My mind tried to figure out just what I would say when asked why I had not been in touch. Pride, shame, sheer terror, all of the above. It was common knowledge they were angry and disappointed; but mostly I had no doubt they felt betrayed. After the phone rang numerous times I realized, as in the hundreds of other times I had called home, I would never have an opportunity to give an excuse.

When I left my car in the company parking lot and entered the taxi with Mr. Major Jasper, not even my fear of flying could be a damper on my joy. Refusing to think of the long flight to Oregon from Atlanta, I only felt like singing, "Free at last, free at last, thank God Almighty I am free at last." Sure that may have unnerved the cab driver and my boss, I made small talk instead. The forty-five minute ride to the airport felt like at least twice that. I anticipated getting away to get out of survival mode. To not have to live like a pauper was all I looked forward to. Knowing I would not have to hide donuts in my purse or hide stolen snacks from the break room at work in the linen closet of our bathroom so I could eat at night was relief all in itself.

By the time we boarded the plane and were securely seated in the business section, my sleepless night wrestled me down like a suspect in a hostage situation. Before the captain introduced himself I was fast asleep. Oddly, the night before my trip, my husband had been meaner than usual. He almost always spoke privately to his mistress, but not that night. Although I knew he did not love me, it was still hard hearing him talk to another woman so X-rated. It had been so long since he touched me, pretended to feel something for me, or even say a kind word to me. Hearing him make promises to her and basically have phone sex with her hurt. Ceasing to salvage my marriage months earlier, I only fought for my sanity and ways to get out.

Anyone looking from the outside in thought we were the perfect couple. He was a contractor with a top secret security clearance with the government and I was an Attorney who worked with one of the largest and most prestigious firms known internationally. We drove fine cars, and wore decent attire; yet the only thing between us was betrayal. I had attempted to leave him several times and bore the scars on my body and my soul of why that wasn't a good idea. He carried a loaded forty-five on him at all times, even when he slept. The same gun had greeted me many times in the wee hours of the morning, reminding me that he owned me and that was the way it would always be. He meant it. Certain the only way I could have any kind of life in this world was if he died, I did the best I could until.

When my boss tapped me on the shoulder I wondered what he could possibly need. Sure I had only dozed, I was shocked to see the mountains and realized the flight was almost over. Mesmerized by the beauty of the city, I sat in silence, awe struck. Feeling peace that I had not known since I realized my husband was a monster, I became emotional. I swear the mountains spoke to me and gave me a new found strength to never stop looking for ways to get out of the hell I called my life. Mr. Jasper dangling a tissue in front of me was when I realized I had shed some renegade tears. He said nothing. I was relieved. My boss was a man of few words and for that I was grateful. We worked together; nothing less, nothing more. He was mission oriented and I was performance oriented so we were a great fit. Our lives, nor did our stories ever intertwine. Just a few inches past average height, the handsome widow, childless, not quite middle aged man had only his career. Oddly that was all I possessed.

My hopes of a mini vacation were short lived. As soon as we arrived at the hotel, Mr. Jasper informed me that we would be having a collaboration meeting in a couple of hours over a late breakfast. All I had to think about was being at home and that thought alone made it easy not to complain. It was after lunchtime at home, but in Portland, Oregon it was only ten in the morning. It was a crisp morning in December that was surprisingly a little warmer than Georgia, but most definitely still quite cold. Elated I had not dressed for fashion but for comfort, I pulled my scarf a little closer to my neck as we entered the second taxi of the day. Although there was less than a thirty minute ride to the hotel, I was overjoyed to finally reach our destination.

My view from the tenth floor of the five star hotel was breathtaking. Standing out in the cold looking over the balcony, all I chose to do was breathe in and breathe out. I was alone. Safe. For at least nine days no one would lift a finger or a fist to hit me. Wanting to shower or at least freshen up a bit, I had to force myself to go inside again. Lifting my suitcase, I was reminded again of my ailing arm. Still very much sore, it protested each time I lifted anything strenuous. It amazed me how one human being could be so cruel to another human being. My husband was calculatingly cleaver in his cruelty that he knew just where to hit me so that my bruises did not show. My face was never a target. He knew people would ask questions. He also knew that later, people would remember if anything ever happened to me. So he only hit what was covered up under my clothing. The purple and black body paintings that told the story of my life were canvased on my milk chocolate skin. The tattooed evidence of a disturbed man displayed all over my back.

By the time I met my boss in the hotel restaurant, I had planned and discarded at least ten escape routes; only to come to realize that the grave was really the only place I had to go. The reality of knowing that all those who were close to me either thought I was crazy or I had turned my back on them for a better life for the man none of them cared for hit hard. My father thought I was disrespectful and my mother worse. The small, close knit circle it took me a decade to build included only myself. When my mother disowned me a part of me had died anyway, so maybe the burial was all that was left. How could I explain that the text messages to them from my cell phone cursing them, and telling them things I would be afraid to ever utter never came from me? I was just as shocked as they were when my mother one day after calling me a liar read a few to me over the phone. I often wondered if my parents ever thought that me, their daughter, using that kind of language all of a sudden was strange. Me telling them that I had moved on and no longer had a use for them because it was time for me to live my life. Telling them to never ask me for money and if I wanted to see them I would come by, otherwise I was just fine should have struck them as outlandish. Even for me. Yes we had words every now and again and sometimes I even came off as selfish and rude, but even that was rare. When those rare moments occurred, I always made things right. I was their only child. The one that took them twenty years and a miracle to conceive. The daughter that if nothing else, respected them for all the sacrifices they had made. Approaching the table where my boss sat looking over the menu, I felt a lot older than twenty-eight.

My life was soon forgotten as the real reason I was in Portland resurfaced. We had our work cut out for us and for the first time in my short career as a lawyer, I wasn't confident about representing a client. Too many unanswered questions. Not enough evidence and too much grief. Airplane crash litigation was tedious at best. So many variables involved. Parts, people, and policies. Our job was to figure out the story. Details spread out among thousands of microscopic pieces. It was difficult knowing the truth and not being able to share it with families who waited at the gates of the airport for loved ones that they would never see again. What was even more difficult was fighting for these people's families and negotiating decent compensation for them while your company tried to cover up and shirk their responsibilities. Knowing what I knew about aviation law and the hazards and cover ups, most people's fear of flying was valid. My problem with the case we currently handled was that the company saw dollar signs, but I saw faces. That was called a conflict of interest so I kept it to myself. Happy I was mostly there to handle the light weight and my boss the senior partner at our office took care of the rest. I felt lucky for once that all of the pressure was not on me.

When Mr. Jasper announced it was quitting time after five straight hours of working nonstop, with the exception of bathroom breaks and coffee, I was relieved. It was short lived. Learning we would resume after dinner in his room was not the news I wanted to hear. Once again I reminded myself that I was not on a holiday but working on a civil case and people's lives depended on the hard work and efforts we made. After revisiting and making some changes to our itinerary, I hurriedly went to my hotel room. Jet lagged and full of mental anguish, I welcomed the serenity of the luxury suite. I was beginning to feel more pain from last night's beating. The pain medication had definitely worn off and all I wanted was a strong drink and a long nap.

When my cell phone rang I suddenly felt sick to my stomach. It was Finn. He rarely called me so I knew it meant trouble. My heart palpitated and my hands became sweaty. Each ring caused me to become more and more anxious until I felt dizzy. All I wanted was to be without him in my life not just for a few days but forever. He was the last person I desired to speak to but what would happen if I did not? Before I could make a decision the room became silent again. It took several minutes before my breathing became normal again. When it did, I made a mental note to lie to him about the call when he asked. My phone did not have reception at the hotel would be my answer. Or maybe I was in a meeting with my boss. Perhaps, I was with a client or out in the field working. Yes, that would work. After all we were going out on site the following day and he knew that was a part of my duties. All I knew was that I had to salvage some peace and speaking to my husband would not bring me anything but hurt and pain. What made me walk into the restroom and intentionally drop my cell phone in the toilet, I do not know; but I felt great afterwards.

3

The next several days were utterly grueling. I was beyond tired and just wanted to enjoy the king sized bed in my hotel room. We worked late into the evenings and then arose early the next day to prepare to meet families, go over reports, and speak with clients. The afternoons were utilized for field visitations, faxing and emailing documents to our head offices. Our rooms looked more like offices than anything else. When my boss gave me a company phone, it was like being pardoned from death row. The company paid the bill and there would be no records for my husband to snoop through because he would never know I had a company phone.

"Mr. Jasper, I am finding some discrepancies in a few of these documents."

It was eleven at night in Oregon but I swear it felt like three in the morning. I was sure my eyes were crossed and no amount of make-up I wore could conceal the bags under them. Without thinking, I removed the jacket I was wearing, not remembering that the top I wore was very low cut in the back. All I knew was that for some odd reason or another, my hotel room was suddenly very warm. That meant either something had gone very wrong with the cooling system or the pain medications I continued to take and the wine I drank were having some weird effect on me. It was not until he did not reply that I became aware that I had made a huge mistake. Without thinking I had allowed him into my sick world. Although my boss and I spent just as much time working in the restaurant as we did in my hotel room, I was still a professional. Him being the gentleman that he was walked the straight and narrow as well. He dressed and behaved in private just as he did in public and so did I. Until my sudden hot flash. Turning around and seeing his white face confirmed that he had seen the scars on my back.

"God in heaven. What happened to you Taylor?"

That was the first time he had ever used my first name. Although he was shocked about what he saw, I was just as shocked at being asked questions about it. All of my answers had always been rehearsed. I was clumsy. I fell. Ran into a door. I had even been mugged a time or two. Those were all answers in my head, but I had never had to use them. No one asked. No one saw. No one really saw. Not knowing what to say, nothing became my response. In a low tone that I had never heard him take with me in the two years we had worked together, he repeated the question in courtroom fashion. "Who did this to you?"

Out of all the ways to react in my mass complicated world of emotions, I never expected to break down and cry. That shocked me, but not as much as his response to my tears. When he turned and walked away my heart sank. But nothing like when he exited through the lock off door between his room and mine. The rejection felt like I had taken a bullet to the head. What had I expected? Maybe I thought someone else finding out about my secret would finally give me the strength to leave. Perhaps I thought I would have some help getting out. Maybe I thought that for the first time in over a year I would not have to carry such a heavy secret. Slumping down on the chase next to my computer I closed my eyes and went into the place I had trained my heart and mind to retreat.

When my boss returned just as he had left the room one hour later, I could tell he had been wrestling with the truth of the real reason for the hatred displayed across my back. When he announced, "Tomorrow you take the day off. I have arranged for the hotel masseuse to come to your room, at your convenience of course. You have worked hard these past few days as always, and I do believe a break is in order. While you enjoy your day, I am going to visit some old friends I have in the area."

I said nothing. Not even a thank you. My thoughts were jumbled and my body was tired. By the time he exited the room again for the final time that night, I believe I was already asleep. For the first time since my life had ended, I was not the only one that carried my secret. Although there had been no words, someone else knew and somehow I found a little consolation in that fact. If I died at my husband's hand someone would know who, why and how.

The knocking on the door alarmed me. I was in a fog and could not get out of it no matter how I tried. I couldn't think. Where was I? I was just unable to put all of the pieces together. The darkness won and I drifted back into the abyss again. I heard voices. They sounded familiar but I could not connect them to a face or a name. Low, muffled, strained voices. Who was in my room? Why was there someone in my room uninvited? Then my heart stopped. My mind said, he's here and he is going to kill you. I sat up in utter terror. I had not made an escape route from the hotel. I figured flying or driving the distance to my hotel would not have been worth it to him. I had been stupid to break my phone. Why had I done something so irresponsible?

"Taylor…Taylor, are you okay?"

The worried sound of my boss's voice registered. Fear still had its grip on me and I felt light headed from my heart racing so fast.

"I had the hotel staff come check on you when you did not contact the masseuse. When I returned from visiting my friends and learned no one had heard from you or seen you I became worried."

Still sick to my stomach I continued to sit in the bed with my head feeling like someone had hit me with a big brick.

"Are you alright? Are you not feeling well?"

My boss continued to fire questions at me and all I could do was breathe in and out. Still in flight mode, I trembled even more. My body did not know what to do or what to feel. It was taking a while to convince myself that I was safe; for the moment anyway.

"You are safe Taylor. He's not here. You are safe, I promise."

The tenderness in his voice made me cry. Tears that I'd held back for far too long came rushing forward. Major Jasper could not handle them.

Clearly nervous and wroth with emotion, he defended his actions. "Please accept my apology. I never meant to startle you; I was just concerned. You did not answer when I left this morning nor this afternoon when I called to make sure you were well. That is when I asked the hotel to check in on you, but they did not receive an answer either. That made me disquieted so I drove back to the hotel to make sure things were as they should be."

Finding my voice I said, "Afternoon?"

"Yes Taylor, it is five in the afternoon."

Dumbfounded at the sound of five, as in I had just slept for nineteen hours straight, sent shockwaves through my body and I began to shake. He moved closer to my bed and took my hand and held it. When I continued to shake he sat on the bed beside me and consoled me. Surprisingly, I did not feel as though I was being forced to do one more thing for the male species. We sat in silence until my stomach growled. Embarrassed I said, "Pardon me."

"Not necessary, you must be famished. Why don't I order some room service?"

"You don't have to do that. I have to shower and dress anyway. I can just find something later.

"It's quite alright. I am a little famished myself."

"Well in that case, I will take a little of everything on the menu." I was joking but not so much. In just a few more days I would be back in Atlanta. Room service was something of a dream for me. Having someone serve me was something of a fantasy and I was going to embellish without any further reservation. When the corners of my boss' lips curved it was shocking. He was such an astute but staid man. Thinking back I doubt I had ever seen him smile very much. It was possible that I had never heard him laugh before.

Trusting him with the matter of dinner, I indulged in a long hot shower. Washing my hair and shaving my legs, I forced myself to think only of the moment. I even took the time to do my monthly self-breast exam while allowing the hot water to baptize me. Each time my husband or my marriage tried to invade my thoughts I forced them out. By the time I emerged from the shower, my hotel room had the aroma of a home cooked meal and I almost ran to the dinner table. The quick second glance at my worn pajamas my boss gave me did not go unnoticed. It did not bother me. For the remainder of the day I was going to be myself. That meant doing a lot of nothing and wearing my favorite pajamas. Should my boss have something to say about them I was ready to defend myself, after all he had given me the day off. My only plans, were having no plans.

"Something smells succulent Mr. Jasper."

"Taylor, I believe it is time you called me Major, and yes it does."

Not responding to his comment, I walked over to see just what room service had delivered. When I removed the cover to the dish and saw the steamed lobster tails and lobster bisque my stomach did several leaps. Unconcerned about how I may have looked to my boss, I immediately took the bread and dipped it into the soup. Closing my eyes, I relished in the perfection that was being intimate with my taste buds. When I opened my eyes I was somewhat embarrassed to see my boss standing there watching me.

"That good aye?"

"Better Mr. Jasper, I mean Major. You must taste it for yourself."

"Well let's eat then."

Taking a seat at the small round table not much was said while I gave great attention to the food placed before me. Although my one hundred and forty pounds did not look like it, I loved food; all kinds of food. Taylor Finn was not, nor had I ever been a picky eater. My boss soon discovered that little fact when he and I reached for the last piece of bread and I quickly grabbed it and took a large bite. When he let out a thunderous laugh he almost startled me. Hearing him laugh like that was odd, but comforting. At least I now knew he had a little bit of humor somewhere deep within him. After placing the tray outside of the door of the hotel room I grabbed the remote with no other intentions other than watching a movie. When I could find nothing interesting to watch I passed the remote control to my boss and he politely placed it on the table. We tried to make small talk about life, but somehow we always ended up discussing work. Neither of us could help ourselves. Heavily engrossed in conversation about some new findings in our case, the time passed unnoticed. Suddenly, around nine that night, there was a booming knock on the door and it immediately sent me into a panic. All I could think of was Finn. He had come to get me. He had come to remind me that I belonged to him and that he would not be ignored or pushed aside. Forgetting that my boss sat right next to me I stood frozen with fear, afraid to say a word.

"Let me check it out Taylor, I'm sure it is nothing."

Reaching out with shaky hands I made an attempt to stop him from going to the door. "No, you fail to understand, I'm supposed to report to him each night, but I haven't. He has to know where I am at all times and I, I, I …out of anger I broke my phone. He hasn't been able to contact me and…I haven't made any efforts to contact him. I just wanted to have a few days without him. It doesn't make sense I know but,…"

"Taylor it makes perfect sense."

Before he could finish his thought there was another knock on the door. Everything inside of me told me that my husband was on the other side of that door and he had come to kill me. My heart and my mind believed nothing else. As I watched Major Jasper, thirty-eight, tall, average build, short black stringy hair that was neatly cut, walk to the door, my parents, and the children I knew I would never give birth to crossed my mind. The video, of my last moments, was that of a woman who had made some choices that had cost her everything. I wanted to stop him. Run. Hide. But where? Maybe it was time I faced my destiny and became what I always knew I would; another statistic. When the door finally opened, I stood waiting. Would he use one of his many guns from his collection? Or maybe he would use his bare hands like I'd dreamed so many times before. The low muffled voices seemed to go on forever. I waited, for the knife, the gun, or even to be pushed over the balcony to my death. There were no last words for me, not even to God. I still did not know for certain if He was real. A part of me just wanted it all to end. The torment, the torture, the heartache, and the depression that plagued me was too much. I closed my eyes and for the first time I wished it would all be over.

Hearing the footsteps and feeling a presence enter the room I did not bother to brace myself. I felt the need to embrace my fate. When I opened my eyes again Mr. Jasper was standing over me. Slumping back onto the couch I was relieved to find a resting place for my wearied body. Neither of us said anything for a while. After the silence became too much for me I looked over at my boss. Our eyes met and when he asked me to, "Tell me what happened to your back." For some unknown reason I did. It was the first time I had ever told the story out loud.

"I thought I had the perfect plan. To start over. My sorority sister, Zoleen helped me. I waited for my husband to go to work one Monday morning and I took what I could and left. Mentally and physically I could not handle one more thing. For the first couple of days it was like heaven. Just to be safe. Being cautious, I never took the same route twice. I changed my schedules and patterns and I purchased a prepaid phone. Then one day I saw him. Standing on the corner of the restaurant where my friend Zoleen and I were sharing a late dinner. He kept his distance. Never said a word and neither did I. After that I would see him outside of my work place. When I came out of the grocery store. Almost everywhere I went. Zoleen thought I was becoming paranoid, but I knew it was him. Just like I knew it was him that night.

He left me there. To die. Or maybe he thought I was already dead. All I knew was that a homeless man found me and flagged down traffic. The gentleman, Lane, said he saw a tall white man dressed in all black run away from the scene. He had heard my screams and followed the sound of my voice. Although the police said he could not make a positive identification of the attacker, without a doubt I could. I knew his voice, his smell, the feel of his hands, and the weight of his foot. I knew everything about him. He was my husband. The man I thought I was not good enough to have. The gift I thought the universe had sent to me.

After being in a coma for eight days I woke up with him sitting by my bedside. He played the doting husband. The perfect man. Always there with me. Helping me to the restroom. Feeding me. Helping me get dressed. Right up to the day we drove away from the hospital. When we pulled into our garage and he turned to me and said, "Don't ever try that again. I will kill you next time, but not before I kill Zoleen, your parents, and even that vendor in your building that is always too nice to you when you pick up your morning coffee. Make no mistake about it, you belong to me. Just look at your back each time you pretend you have forgotten."

From that point on I became his slave. He sleeps in the master bedroom and I sleep in the guest bedroom. I prepare his meals. Clean our home and do whatever else he orders me to do. He gave me a new phone. Made me change all of my bank account information online so he could have access to it. If he feels like I am worthy of eating he allows it. If not, I starve. He times me when I go to work and when I come home. If I am late, I get a beating. If I do not prepare his food correctly, he hits me. If he has a disagreement with his mistress, he makes sure I am miserable because of it."

The words, bouncing off the walls of the hotel room were painful. Heartbreaking. Even to me it was hard to hear and I already knew my story. At least the story from my side of the pages. Who really knew what went through an abusers head. The mind of a murderer. A child molester. An adulterer. A rapist. Did Hitler decide over breakfast one day to put millions of innocent people in a gas chamber? Was it the first thought of little Jeffery to have people for lunch the first opportunity made available to him. Did America plan to have slaves? And then be so cruel to them? I shuddered even attempting to imagine the vile thoughts and reasoning of such evil deeds.

For my boss, my story must have been hard to hear because he reached out to me. "May I hold you?" He did not wait for an answer. He pulled me to him so that the weight of my body leaned against him and the only thing left for me to do was to put my head on his shoulder. I was too scared to say no. He was my boss. A great boss, but still my boss. He was ten years my senior and I had no idea what he wanted other than to try and console me. He just could not understand that it was much too late for consolation. When he took his hand and softly pushed my head on his shoulder I did not protest. I was used to men forcing me to do what they wanted me to. After all, he was my boss, and I needed my job.

When he kissed me I did not pull away. I did not love him. I did not even know him. I did not know what diseases he might have. If he had a significant other or if he went home to a pet. It had been so long since I had been touched, made love to or the better term was, had sex. I was married. There was no justification in doing the same thing to my husband that he was doing to me. It was nice and slow--- easy like the gentle cool rain on an early spring morning. He led and I followed. His eyes never left mine until he saw in them that I had experienced some pleasure in the cruel life in which I lived. The way he served me and touched me; I had the feeling that he had become my protector. He did not stay the night, but kissed me and quietly left me with my thoughts.

Holding onto the pillow, my feelings of comfort were short lived. I had just had sex with a man because he was nice to me. I had forgotten what kindness looked and felt like. My parents had cut me off because I had married a white man. There was so much racial tension in the country. With such clearly defined lines of hatred by a few of those who were supposed to protect and some others in authority, my parents felt I had betrayed our culture. All I knew was that someone had cared. I had no idea where my job stood, what my future held, or if I should have guilt. To my heart, Portland was all I had.

The next several days consisted of working over breakfast, slaving over lunch, and making love over dinner. Major always left shortly afterwards. Until one night the loneliness, the emptiness, and the fear became overwhelming. That night, just as in all the others, we laid naked in the darkness consumed by the silence. He got up to leave and something inside of me broke. Maybe it was already broken, but in that moment, I knew I could not go through life alone. When I said, "Stay", he stopped in mid motion. When he switched on the light I will never know what he was looking for. I can only guess that he found it because he never said a word but pulled back the covers and reentered my bed. I wanted to thank him for staying, but when I turned to do so he was already fast asleep. From that time on our relationship changed. He did things for me and to me that I never dreamt. By day he was my boss and well sought after attorney. By night he was the man that made me feel like a woman again. Like I had value. Was beautiful. Was wanted for more than the check that was deposited into my bank account biweekly. One night he asked me if I needed anything. The question surprised me. My answer surprised me even more. "Just you Major." It was obvious my answer pleased him.

4

When Major touched my hand and squeezed it just before our plane landed, I had a heart full of sorrow. I did not want to go home. Our last night together had consisted of him begging me to allow him to put me in a safe house somewhere. There was no doubt in my mind that there was no such place. Finally giving up on the idea to hide me, my lover decided to arm me. We had code words that only he and I would understand. I had a key to his apartment for emergency shelter. He purchased a phone for me that no one could track and put minutes on it so that I would never have to feel I was alone. He added money to a reloadable Visa card for me that was neatly hidden along with the other items he had given to me.

The drive from the airport was the longest I had ever traveled. I turned around three times to go the designated meeting place chosen by Major and I to see one another. Halfway to my prison cell Major called but I did not answer. I could not hear his voice because I would abandon all reason and run to him. Speaking to him would make me weak and that would kill me. Having allowed my heart out made me vulnerable; too vulnerable. Finn would be livid and that scared me. We had not spoken since the day I destroyed my phone. He had no idea when I was coming home and walking into that kind uncertainty I did not know what to expect. I was sure that he would punish me. Not knowing how gave me more grief. Would he make me sit in hot water like I had before? Maybe he would pour bleach on all my clothes and then make me wash and fold them, just to throw them away afterwards. Whatever his punishment, I put my heart and my mind in a safe place so I could endure it.

I braced myself when I entered my home after being gone for almost two weeks. The alarm system had not chimed and that immediately triggered fear. Terror that almost made me turn around and run. Knowing my husband would be waiting somewhere to hit me for some unknown reason made me edgy. His car was parked in the driveway so I knew he was at home, waiting. Almost tiptoeing through the house I cautiously went around each corner. Something did not feel right. My house had a stench. The odor of something foul reeked in the air. The television could be heard from the study that I was rarely allowed to visit. The door was closed. Standing outside the door I was too terrified to open it; yet more fearful of not greeting him in my home coming. I knocked. No answer. I called out, "Finn...Finn, I just wanted to tell you that I was home." No answer. Certain not opening the door would bring me more harm, I reluctantly pushed it open. Overtaken by the smell I became nauseous. The room was dark and the blinds closed; something Finn hated, especially in the afternoon. He loved to see the afternoon sunlight reflect on the Tiffany lamp on his desk. Holding my nose with one hand, I flicked on the light with the other and my heart stopped.

There slumped over in the chair was my husband. Lifeless. His rigor mortis body was still dressed in work clothes that were soiled with blood. Losing complete control of my bodily functions I begin vomiting and hyperventilating. Leaving a trail of my insides as I ran, I felt like I would faint at any minute. My brain was screaming, "My husband is dead. Dead. He is dead, in our house." Maybe the killer was still there. Would they come back for me? What? Who? My mind ran as fast as my legs did to the house almost an entire block away. When I reached the neighbor's home, all I could do was make up sign language when Mr. Willard finally answered my constant banging.

"June, you had better get out here! Something is wrong."

"What is it Walter?" Mrs. Willard dropped the plate she had been drying when she saw my face and my soiled cotton gray pants. "Oh sweet God Almighty, what's wrong child!"

She shook me attempting to receive some kind of response but I only dry heaved and pointed. That was when she grabbed my hand and began to run towards my home. Mr. Willard, and their dog, Billy, ran right behind us. Once we entered my home, I refused to go any further. I could not see him like that again. As much as I hated what he had done to me, I still could not bear to see him that way. Still unable to speak, I pointed to the back of the house. Mr. Willard knew something was amiss and instructed his wife not to move. Cautiously proceeding down the hall I knew, we both knew when Mr. Willard first saw what I did and smelled what I had. Hearing him chant, "The Lord is my shepherd, I shall not want. He makes me to lie down in green pastures…" The sound of her husband praying as if giving a eulogy sent Naomi Willard into protective mode.

"Walter I'm coming in there right now."

"No Naomi, you stay right where you are and I mean it." The tone of his voice halted her in her steps.

I listened as Mr. Willard spoke into his cell phone to the 911 operator. Giving my home address and then graphic details of the scene, I hovered in the corner of the living room floor rocking back and forth. Mrs. Willard attempted to console me by rubbing my back, but it was clear she needed to be consoled herself. Judging from the bullet to my husband's head, there was no doubt about it, someone had murdered him. Someone had been in our home and executed him and my entire being was shaken.

By the time the police arrived I was breathing in and out of a brown paper bag at Mrs. Willard's demand. The concern for me mirrored in both of my neighbors' eyes, but it could not touch the sorrow in my heart. Still in the soiled clothing and dry heaving I watched as in a slow motioned horror film as the paramedics, the ambulance, the police, and lastly the coroner infiltrated my home. The police asked me all sorts of questions that I just did not have the answers to give to them. Maybe even if I had been qualified enough to speak about the situation, my mental capacities had shut down. Seeing the officers and my neighbors whisper, it did not take a genius to figure out that they were discussing me. One of the officers nonchalantly says, "Maybe she should be taken in. She doesn't look too good." All thought it to be a great idea. I wanted to protest, but found it difficult to instruct my brain to commute such an argument. It wasn't until they all gathered around me, planning to carry out the officer's plan to have me taken to the mental ward, did I wake up. Screaming at no one in particular I insisted they,

"Leave me alone." I screamed it until I had no voice and what little strength I had was gone.

When I came out of my conniption, Mrs. Willard was softly crying and Mr. Willard stood guard over me like a lion guarding his cubs. Not understanding my surroundings, I had no idea I had lost several minutes of my life. I could only be told what actually transpired. It did not take long for me to figure out what was taking place. I was an attorney. I was well aware of the routine. Atlanta's finest wanted to question me and would not leave until the wife of the deceased had given them the answers they sought.

It was several hours later before I would find myself alone. Too afraid to shower, to drive, or even to leave the living room, I stood in the middle of the living room floor shaking uncontrollably. Not knowing what to do, I figured that I should call someone to tell them that Finn had been taken from this world. His parents would want to know, maybe. His job would need to know. But that was not an easy task. Finn did not have a real relationship with his family. It was all surface. I did not even know of a way to contact them. His phone had a password on it that he had never shared with me. I had not seen any of his family since our wedding day. His half-sister was employed at a local bank, but no bank was open at night. My heart was longing to speak to Major. I felt it to be disrespectful to the dead, no matter how awful of a husband he had been to me. The only thing I was certain of was that I could not, would not, sleep in the home I had shared with my husband for such a short time.

After I drove around my boss' neighborhood for the fifth time, I finally decided to check into a hotel for the night.

All I had was the clothing that I had traveled to Portland with, nothing else. Taking a few minutes before leaving my home to dispose of my soiled clothing and change, I had hurriedly grabbed my bag and left. The thoughts of what happened to Finn were thrusting me out the door. Paranoid, I walked into the hotel only to learn that there were no vacancies. Exhausted, jet lagged and in a state of shock, I left the hotel parking lot realizing I did not have a friend in the world. Those very thoughts weighed heavy on me; to the point that I became paralyzed with anxiety and was forced to pull to the side of the road for the sake of my safety. I couldn't breathe. My heart raced and I felt as though I would die. Die, alone on the side of the freeway. My parents were all I could think of. I longed to talk to them. Find refuge in my daddy's house. My mother's food. If only I could hide in the bedroom that had not changed since my high school years. I tried dialing their number from the secret phone that was intended for only Major and I, but no answer. When the phone rang almost as quickly as I placed it in the cup holder, my heart leaped. Not needing to look at the number I immediately answered the call.

"Hello."

"Hi, I have been worried about you."

Hearing Major's voice caused me to break once again. My nerves were seared and it became obvious to him when I began to cry and speak incoherently. In the calm manner that was only Major Jasper, he took control.

"Breathe Taylor. Breathe."

Obeying his orders I allowed air to pass through my lungs.

"Where are you?"

"On the expressway."

"Where Taylor?"

"Ferguson and Meadows."

"Just keep breathing and I will be there shortly."

"But you don't understand. I won't be here when you get here. It's my time. I know it."

"No Taylor. You will be just fine. Close your eyes."

"No Major, listen. Please promise me that you will find my parents. Tell them that they were correct about everything. Tell them that I am so sorry for the pain I caused them. That I love them more than life itself."

"You are going to tell them those words Taylor. Now close your eyes like I asked you to do."

There is a pause and then he comes back again. "Are they closed?"

"Yes."

"Imagine you are on the final push after several hours in labor. You hear the counting. One, two, three, four, five, six, seven, eight, and then all of a sudden you feel the moment you have longed for since you played with your dolls as a little girl. The nurse says, "It's a boy" and she places him on top of you as he is cleaned. Then you hear the most amazing sound you have ever heard as your son cries. You look down at him and immediately fall in love with him. You memorize every detail of his face with one glance. You know in that instant that you would die for him. When he continues to cry you tell him, "It's okay son. Mommy is here. I have you." You take him in your arms. You kiss him and promise him that you will always be there for him no matter what happens. You can never imagine, from the time you first see him, how you could ever live your life without him. You are a mother. What you have dreamt of being. What you were born to be. You are a mother because you survived. You overcame. You conquered. You won." There is a pause. "Do you see him Taylor? Do you see how beautiful he is? How perfect he is? How happy you are? Fulfilled? Satisfied? Do you Taylor?"

"Yes. I see him."

"Open the door Taylor."

"How do I do that Major? I don't know how to get there from here."

"Open the door my love."

"I don't understand. Tell me how Major."

"Just open your eyes and open the door. You are safe now."

Seeing him standing there in front of my door on the side of the interstate in the middle of the night was the best thing that had happened to me in a long time. I believe that was when I fell in love with Major Jasper.

5

By the time I entered the home of Major Jasper on the
North side of town, he knew everything that I did about my
husband's death. He decided that it would be best to leave
my car behind and I had not argued with him. My body was
being sustained on zero hours of sleep, having been up for
twenty-four hours. Mentally I was spent and physically it
was worse. I had a funeral to plan. A family to locate and a
mind to keep stable. All of which seemed impossible for a
victim of domestic violence and now a widow of a man that
was without a doubt murdered in cold blood.

When I showered I felt the need to wash every part of my
body excessively. My mind replayed the scene at my home
repetitively. Nothing I did had the power to mute the replay
button. After being in the shower for an hour, the sound of
my name disconcerted me. Eventually concluding it was
Major, I emerged from the shower very reluctantly. Heavily
weighed down with fear, grief, and hopelessness, I walked
straight into the towel he held open for me. My breaking
point was at hand and we were both privy to that
appointment. Not bothering to dress I followed his lead. I
wasn't concerned by where we would end up. Any place
was better than where I currently resided. Making no fuss
at all, I willingly went through the bedroom that I assumed
was his. As he undressed I stood next to the bed and
waited. When he pulled back the covers and motioned for
me to go in first I obeyed. That is where I stared at the wall
for the next three hours. Every sound terrified me. Each
noise caused me to almost go into hysteria. When Major's
arms could not console me, his kisses did not make me

forget, and his words went unheard he left the bed. I could hear him in the kitchen. Even knowing he was not far away my body still trembled with fear. After several minutes of torture he hovered over the bed.

"Drink this Taylor."

His voice left no room for me to question him. I did not. Putting the glass to my mouth I could smell a strong odor but dared not comment on it. The taste initially caused me to grimace and immediately stop drinking.

"I would never hurt you Taylor. Finish it." Although his voice was low, it was monotone, and authoritative. Having heard it countless times dealing with clients, I understood it was his voice that would not reason. Throwing back my head I forced myself to do as he instructed. He cordially took the glass and placed it on the bookshelf and joined me in the bed again. My body continued to shake with anxiety for a little while.

"You are safe Taylor. I promise. I will never allow anyone else to hurt you. Never. Just close your eyes and rest now. We will figure out tomorrow when it comes."

Wanting to believe him for all of ten seconds I soon dismissed any such promise. No man had ever protected me. Not even my father. Whatever my mother decided he had gone along with despite how much it hurt our family. That was the ultimate reason I was only attracted to strong men. Take charge, rough around the edges, rebel men that would never allow anyone to lead them around by the nose. That plan had backfired royally.

Talking into the darkness I listened as Major Jasper did everything in his power to make me better. The truth was, I was feeling more relaxed. Whether or not it was a medicated induced calm did not matter. My shaking ceased and something else woke up inside of me. An appetite that demanded it be fed and Major was the only food that would suffice. My need for him was so overwhelming that I grabbed a handful of his hair and pulled his head down to me and French kissed him like I had no knowledge I could. When I rolled over on top of him and began to kiss him in places he had not imagined, I was positive I shocked him. All of the pent up frustrations and the uncertainty of my future came out as I touched, teased, and taunted his body in X-rated pleasure. It was the first time we had actually been together. All of the other times we had sex he was trying to make me feel better. This time I needed to relieve myself of everything that troubled me. He was my treadmill and I rode him until I could not go anymore. When I collapsed from exhaustion he caught me and finished the remainder of the marathon.

When daylight crept into the bedroom bringing all the darkness of the previous day once again, I clothed myself in it. The thoughts of making burial arrangements for Finn, notifying his family, and returning to the home we had shared petrified me. Not knowing what or who happened to him made me mentally and physically ill. I never wanted to venture outside again. Grateful it was Saturday, work was something I could put on hold until I found the strength to face the destiny that had chosen me. Finn was such a private person I had no idea where to find the insurance policies. I needed to find an apartment. I would not assume that Major and I would live together. Going to the police station was high on my list of priorities. Were there any suspects? When had my husband been killed? Why had he been murdered? Why had it taken place in our home? Question after question danced ballet on my brain. My insides hurt. My stomach felt sick and I wanted to run and hide in my lower self but even that part of me was comatose.

"Don't Taylor. I won't allow you to do this alone."

Shocked that Major felt my thoughts, our eyes met in a battle. Mine with defiance of the invasion of my privacy and his with the determination that he would take charge whether I wished him to or not. Softening a bit, he touched my face.

"There is not anything that I would not do for you Taylor. Anything."

Something about his statement thrilled me and alarmed me at the same time. Staring at his face I wondered if I was just being paranoid or if for the first time I saw darkness in him.

"I have to go home soon Major. I need to make burial arrangements or see if perhaps he has already made those preparations. To find his will."

"Not alone. I will be at your side."

Swallowing, I made mental deliberations on telling my lover that he should not be present as I buried my husband. No matter how abusive he had been to me. The only person I had ever trusted with that information had been him. My abuse had been only a matter of my husband and the universe. The pregnant pause allowed him time to solidify his vow to me.

"You were his wife in name only. He was a coward and I feel no remorse that he will never harm you again. You did not deserve that and you know it. When you bury him, I will be there. When you decide what you want to do about the home you shared with him, I will be there." Taking my hand in his, the gray eyes that I was still learning to read stared into mine. I had no doubt he was closing the case. Deciding to revisit the conversation when I had a stronger rebuttal I only nodded in response. Leaning back on the pillow again intending to make a mental to do list, it shocked me when Major began to speak again. Not that he spoke, but what he spoke.

"I love you Taylor and I will always protect you."

My heart raced. Love. We never spoke of love. We never planned anything outside of spending the night together. He was my secret safe place and beyond that we had not decided. Sure he had begun to take care of me rather quickly. No, I had never refused his willingness to be my everything. I liked the attention. It gave me great satisfaction and a feeling of power to know that I could make a man forget his life to be a part of mine. I smiled in the dark each time he cried out my name when we made love. Each text I received strengthened my self-esteem. Whereas I had been nothing to Finn, it felt liberating to become someone's everything. That is when I decided that love would not matter to me any longer. As long as he wanted to give me his all, I would take it. Knowing that he waited for me to reply I opened my eyes and walked into my future.

"You are the best thing that has ever happened to me Major Jasper. My lover and my friend. When I am with you I know I am safe. When you touch me I am satisfied. You are all I ever want for the rest of my life."

I saw the change come over him. The pleasure in his eyes at my words. The way his body succumbed to my words and the instant when he opened a place for me to enter in that I was sure no other woman had ever possessed. To me it was like giving blood to a vampire. I salivated at the fact that I could control this man after being controlled by all others all of my life. Not waiting for him to kiss me, once again I took charge. Putting my head under the covers I taught him things he never knew about his body. Positions he had no idea existed. I led, he followed; until I was sure he would want no other woman. Need no other touch. Voice. Just like Finn had owned me, I had to own Major. It was the only way I could ensure my safety. I felt his heart race, his body tremble. Just when he needed to enter in I whispered in his ear, "Please don't ever let me go my love or I will die." The room exploded and my soul became sealed to Major Jasper, good or bad.

Through his heavy breathing he forced out, "There is no going back Taylor. You are mine now. Forever."

That should have made me afraid, but it did not. I had been owned before. At least this time I had chosen how I would wear my shackles.

6

Hearing everyone speak well of Finn made me nauseous.
Not one week had passed that he had not beaten me. Not
one day that he had not called me names that raped my self-
esteem and brutally assassin my character and mutilated my
being. Even in his death he took careful concern to reiterate
the message that I was nothing to him. There was the cars
and a summer beach home where they met often that I
never knew existed. There was some property in another
state where he was planning to relocate. And a restaurant
he was part owner of, and it all belonged to his mistress.
The only thing I had was the home we shared together. It
was mine; mortgage and all. All of his life insurance
policies had listed her as the beneficiary. Every part of his
estate that he could legally transfer had been handed to her
on a silver platter, along with my dignity. Marlo Santeen
Miller was now a wealthy woman. The bitterness in my
heart made it easy not to shed a tear for the monster in the
casket that was stretched out before me. Having to become
in debt to a funeral home to bury the man that had not
thought enough of me to even take care of his own burial
services was enough to make me walk up to the casket and
kill him again.

Sitting on the front row alone with Finn's family was
awkward. They had decided to bury him in the family plot
and I had not argued. There were no plans in my future to
ever visit him there. The Bardo family, unknown to me,
was very well off. Old money and chosen life styles. It had
been shocking to learn that all of them knew about Marlo
and had embraced her as one of them. She and Finn had a

history. One that everyone except Finn's grandfather, the one that controlled the estate approved. Little did I know, until Finn's sister and best friend to Marlo had been so willing to share with me. I learned that Finn's grandfather had placed a condition on him receiving his inheritance. He would have to marry, and remain married for two years to someone other than the love of his life and mistress. To Finn Bardo I had only been a pawn. He had chosen me as his wife because he and his sister decided the first woman he encountered that day would be his wife. That person had been me. To them I had only been an object. A means to get where he wanted to be in life. For that I hated all of them. His death for me was karma's pay back for all the evil deeds he had done. All I had to do was get through the funeral service.

Knowing I wasn't alone there with them was enough to keep my head held in pride. Major sat on the last row to the chapel, ready to come to my rescue at a moment's notice. Soon after all of this sordid mess was over we were going to be married. I was going to give him the children he wanted and spend the rest of my life being comfortable. Finn had not won after all. Major was all I had and I would make sure that it remained that way.

Walking up to the bronze casket and looking down at the man I never knew was more than I imagined it would be. He looked as though he slept. The scar from the bullet to his head was hidden under is black hair. There was a stern look on his face. One that I had seen often. Too often. One part of me was burying a total stranger. The other part, the one that I had given to him in marriage, grieved for what we never had. The fairytale that I believed could be mine from the moment I first laid eyes on him. My mind went over and over the last time I'd seen him watching me drive away. That last phone call to me. What had he wanted? The fool in me hoped maybe he just wanted to talk. Like in the beginning, but then I remembered none of that had been real. It was all a game to gain my trust so I would marry him and he could eventually wed the woman he truly loved. When the funeral director took my arm and attempted to guide me in the direction of the exit, I figured I had been standing over Finn's body for too long. I still did not move. All of the pain from our broken relationship came rushing forth. The beatings. The mental anguish. The weekends without eating. Months of not seeing my family or friends. I wanted to yell at him. Ask him how he could treat me that way? Feeling the hot salty tears that sprinkled my lips were not an indicator of what could have been, but what should have never been.

When the services were over, I rode in the car alone. The only person that acknowledged me was Mr. Bardo; Finley Bardo, the infamous grandfather. Portable oxygen tank, large glasses, and frail frame, he stood powerfully over all at the graveside. Whether or not it was his money that made all stand at his attention and bowed at his authority, I followed suit when he summoned me.

"Mrs. Bardo, I expect for you to meet with me two weeks from today. September 25th, at the Roselee Estate on Harper road. Wednesday morning, eleven o'clock." Giving me a card he continues, "Call my office for directions if need be. I do not like stragglers."

With his southern accent being very distinct, I listened closely to him as he spoke to make sure I understood him. When he was done speaking he motioned for the car to be brought around and then he was gone. The remainder of the Bardos stared at me and whispered. Some even made gestures, but mostly they comforted Finn's poor grieving mistress as his wife looked on.

Life was cruel. No matter how things ended with my husband, I loved him with all of my heart in the beginning. He was my everything. Although I was just a game to him, it still did something to me the way everything ended. I would never be able to ask him why he did the things to me that he had done. Seeing them lower his body into the ground with so many questions remaining unanswered cause the salty tears to return. I could live with not knowing the whys. Looking at his mistress and the way the family adored her, that mystery was already solved. He did not love me. Had never loved me. Still, there was the matter of a "who" that me and the Atlanta police department wanted to know. Who was your murderer Finn Bardo? That was all I thought about. It had me looking over my shoulders. Waking up in the middle of the night with cold chills despite my lover's firm grip.

7

The ride home was a quite one. Deep in thought I did not
really notice that something had disturbed Major.
Assuming he was giving me the time I needed to process
the funeral I welcomed the quietness. It wasn't until we
arrived home that I learned otherwise. When I asked him if
he would be okay with me going to bed because I was
exhausted he did not answer.

"Did you hear me Major?"

Never would I have believed his response to me.

"How could you still be in love with him?"

"Excuse me."

"Your late husband. How could you love him after all he
did to you?"

"Where on earth would you get that idea Major?"

"You cried for him at the service today. I saw you
heartbroken, standing over his casket."

"That doesn't mean I love him. I don't know; it is hard to
explain. We were married. As evil as he was to me, he was
still a human being. Someone put a bullet in his head in our
home and left him there knowing he had a wife. It is a lot to
comprehend Major. So much to deal with all at one time.
My emotions and my mind are on overload and I cannot
stop it."

When he opened my car door, held my hand as we walked through the garage, and into the house without saying a word I knew he was still upset. With Major I had learned quickly what to do to make him better. His pressure points and his pleasure points were not hard to discover. He had trigger words that I only needed to whisper and he was willing to forget what made him disgruntled. On a normal day, feeding into his ego would have been too easy. The day I buried my husband was a whole different story.

Finding the first resting place I could, I sat down in a leather recliner in the living room. He sat opposite of me on the couch. Neither of us said anything. After sitting in silence for a while my nerves could not handle the atmosphere any longer. Deciding to change my clothing, I left the room. How could I make him understand? Not feeling anything at all would make me just as much of a monster as my late husband had been. Planning nothing more than to put on something comfortable, my body hit a new level of exhaustion and I took refuge in the bed. When Major came into the bedroom several minutes later neither of us spoke. I studied his face when he wasn't looking. The soft features of the almost forty year old made anyone feel at home. His twinkling, almost translucent gray eyes were welcoming. His freshly cut black hair was the same as it always was, but he was not. His weight on the bed felt heavy to my soul and I just needed some space to think. Wanting to get up and leave the room I stared up at the ceiling. If I left he would become more offended and that would in no way help resolve any issues. He needed to know that I was his. That he would not have to compete with a dead man. That my loyalty was his and his alone.

Despite my fatigued mind, exhausted body, and crippled soul, I rolled over to where he sat on the bed and reassured him.

"You are my love." Putting my head in his lap I continued. "Never do I want to think of being without you or losing you. The only reason I made it through the service today was because I knew you were there."

He said nothing. The thought of us having our first spat, at the worst possible time was more than I could handle. Bursting into tears I ran from the room. Having no idea where to find solace I tried to escape to the backyard, but fumbled with unlocking the door. I never heard his footsteps behind me.

"Please don't run away from me. I want you to always know you can run to me."

He pleaded, but I was too distraught to give way to the dismay in his voice. Angrily, I yelled, "Then do not push me away! You said I could trust you. Then you turn around and judge me because I have feeling. I have never been here before. All of this is new for me and it is hard to handle."

Crying uncontrollably, I still fumbled with the door. Getting away from the walls that seemed to be closing in on me so I could breathe was my only thought. From behind I felt his arms go around my waist, his body press hard against my body and his lips brushed my neck.

"Forgive me, please, my sweet Taylor."

Still very upset I reminded him. "You were supposed to be my secret place. My safe place. You promised! You promised me Major Oswald Jasper."

Turning me to him, he begged me to forgive him again. Feeling so overwhelmed all I could do was weep violently. Foolishly he made a futile effort to wipe each tear away. Still kissing me he repeatedly tells me he loves me. He would never hurt me. I believed him and collapsed in his arms. That is where we stood, locked in each other's arms by the back entrance to his one story cottage home.

"I love you Taylor Denise Jasper. More than anything."

Hearing Major address me, as though I was already his wife, in a moment of raw passion was like water to my thirsty soul. Becoming even more emotional I kissed him back the way he desired to be kissed. He picked up my one hundred and forty pound body with ease and carried me to the same bedroom that I had run from minutes earlier. I never stopped kissing him, touching him. Just before he lowered me to the bed I uttered to him, "I love you Major." For just one instant he froze. Wanting to make sure he heard me I repeated myself. "I love you so much it hurts."

When he abruptly pushed me away I searched his eyes for an explanation, only to learn that he was searching mine. He wanted, needed something more. I attempted to give it to him.

"Please do not make me wait any longer my love. I want you Major. I need you, now."

"Say it again my sweet. I have to look at you when you do."

Obeying him, our eyes locked and I said once more, "I love you and you are the only man I want to be with."

Before the words were completely out of my mouth he was already proving his love to me. Over and over again. The walls of the room absorbed the moans and groans of two people that just needed someone to love them. Someone to be there. Whatever way he desired for me to love on him I did. I yearned for him to make me forget about the last few months of my life; he did. When I screamed, a sound he had not heard, then and only then did he allow himself to reach his point of no return.

Afterwards, I continued to kiss him. "Oh Major, I love you so much. You make me feel so good. Please don't push me away. Even if I've been naughty, love me anyway."

Unsure what had come over me, I would not stop caressing his head, rubbing my finger across his lips, and nibbling on his ear. He appeared to have gone away from me and it frightened me. When at last I heard the sound of his voice, I felt relief. Our bodies were still intertwined and hearts racing when he told me what he imagined I was reluctant to hear.

"Taylor I know we promised to wait to be married, but that is a vow I am unable to keep. Waiting to make you mine is something I am unable to do." Taking my left hand in his he removed the wedding band and placed it on the nightstand next to the bed. "Marry me Taylor. Don't make me wait any longer."

Knowing that to anyone looking on my actions would be scandalous. Time was what I really needed. Everything was happening so fast. In less than a month I went from being a victim of domestic and mental abuse, to adulterer, to widow, and now he proposed marriage. He was what I wanted, but in the right time and season. Instead of conveying that message to him in hopes that he would understand I went with my raw emotions.

"Whenever you are ready my love, I want to be your wife."

That pleased him. It pleased me. I had another shot at happiness and I was going to take it. Who were we hurting? Finn was dead.

8

Having taken a leave of absence for the next month from my firm to bury my husband and get my life in order, I found myself staring out of the window most of the day. Sixty days was what I had to decide what to do with the house. On my list of top priorities was finding another place of employment. Major decided it would be best and I agreed. Especially with the recent events of my life. Clients might find it hard to trust the integrity of an attorney who moved the widow of a murdered man right into his home with no remorse. We decided to wait until the case was closed before getting married. That was my idea. I believed it would not take too long. I called the police station, but they still had no leads. Major wanted children right away and I planned to give them to him. He wasn't aware of it, but I was already off the pill. Figuring it would take a few weeks to get the birth control out of my system I gave my body a head start. The only thing I had left to do was settle my late husband's estate and that would be accomplished the following day when I met with his grandfather, Finley Bardo.

When I drove up to the Rosalee Estate I was memorized. The place looked like it was something out of a magazine. Not what I expected at all. Hidden away in the countryside of Atlanta was a world all of its own. It was 10:59 in the morning and I had broken every state law there was trying to make my eleven o'clock appointment on time. Traffic had been brutal. My hair unmanageable, and Major's temper juvenile. He had not wanted me to come. Feeling ousted by my continued connection with the Bardo family, but something within me knew I had to meet with Finley Bardo at any cost.

Sure that I pulled into the drive of the estate on two wheels, I threw the car into park and sprinted to the first entrance I could find. There were so many it was like playing guess who. Just when I was about to knock on the door, it opened and a woman of color greeted me.

"Taylor Bardo follow me please."

Dressed in a plain black dress she wasted no time with formal greetings but hurried me down the hall to a huge office. One like we would conduct deliberations for a case. Not having time to process whether she was rude or right, before I could think of anything to say I stood face to face with Mr. Finley Bardo.

"Mrs. Bardo I believe I made it clear to you that your timeliness would be appreciated."

Instantly angry, I fired off, "Mr. Bardo, with all due respect, it is eleven o'clock. If my memory serves me correctly, that is the time of my appointment."

Looking at me through his large glasses intently he fires right back at me. "You are late Mrs. Bardo. On time is always late in this world. Remember that."

Judging him and sending him straight to hell by my standards I regretted not listening to Major. Getting up to leave I decided that I had been abused by my last Bardo. Wanting to throw something at his big bald head before leaving I only said, "Thank you for your time." That is when he said, "Sit down Taylor Bardo. We have business." He instructed my escort to his office to close the door behind her on her way out. I was almost afraid. What kind of business could he have with me? Finn had not left me one thing in his will. Until the day of the funeral I had not ever met him and for that I was grateful. When the door closed behind "Beatrice Blue" the room fell still, until my phone rang and I wanted to die. Knowing it was Major checking on me because I had promised to tell him when I arrived, I was embarrassed to pick it up. When Mr. Bardo ordered me to, "Shut that thing off," I wanted to throw it at him. Glaring at him I obeyed.

"Shall we get down to business Mrs. Bardo or would you like to take lunch now?"

His sarcastic manner was close to making me commit murder. I figured we had better handle whatever business he had with me so I could be done with the entire Bardo zoo. Nodding my head in a professional manner I assured him I was ready to get started.

"Good. It has come to my attention that there are some matters in which your late husband has been negligent."

Not having a clue as to what matters he referred to, I listened intently.

"My grandson was the joint heir to the Bardo estate in the event of my death Mrs. Bardo. Any children born to him would have shared his inheritance. Finn would only have inherited his estate if and when he married and remained married for a specified amount of time. That time requirement had not been satisfied when he was so tragically taken from our family."

Listening attentively I wondered what any of it had to do with me. We had no children. Finn made certain of that. I now knew why. Up until his death I had no clue Finn was wealthy. The way he spent and controlled my earnings had not made any sense to me until I realized that was the way he kept me with him. If I had no means I could not start over. Especially with no family connections or friends. When I checked back in from my mental sabbatical, I realized that Mr. Bardo had asked me a question for which he awaited an answer. Embarrassed, I could only say, "Excuse me sir, would you repeat the question please."

Glaring at me he allowed us to sit in an awkward silence for several minutes. Minutes that made me livid. So livid I stood up and let him have it.

"Why did you bring me here to insult me? To belittle me? You Bardo's are experts at making others feel inferior to you. I never asked to come here. I do not know you or any of the other Bardo family members but I did know Finn. Or at least I thought I did. He was the husband I only dreamed of marrying and sharing the rest of my life. Until he began to beat me senseless every time he felt like it. Even so, it was still the worse day of my life finding him that way. In our home. No answers as to who or why. Burying him, especially when I learned he did not love me, and never had. That I was just a pawn in some sick game he was playing. Do you know what that feels like? Do you care? Your grandson had a mistress the entire time we were married. He left everything he owned to her. I will be paying for his funeral for the rest of my life. Living with the scars he placed on my body and my soul until I die. Was that not enough for you people? Then you bring me here to humiliate me. No, no, no. I will not have any further dealings with this family. Good day to you Mister Bardo!"

Literally running from the room I never looked back at the old man sitting at the huge oval desk.

The first thing I did once in my car was call Major. When he answered I had no words. All I could do was sob in the phone. He didn't say much but I knew he was there for me and that was all I needed to know. When I pulled into the driveway, to my surprise he was waiting for me; his arms and his love. We were beginning our life together and putting the past behind us.

9

Needing to feel like I belonged somewhere I forced myself up from the couch that had become my daily prison. When Major came home he would not have to ask me about the clothes that still remained in the suitcases on the floor in the closet. Those clothes would be put away nicely and neatly and more of me would infiltrate the home that was becoming ours.

It had been three months since Finn's death and the fact that the case was still open bothered me more than I led on. From time to time I drove by the house, but I still could not go in. With the part time job I had managed to obtain I was able to pay the mortgage and keep the utilities on. Finn took care of all my needs, except that one. Adamant about why I still held on to the house, he made it clear in no uncertain terms that he could not support me financially in such a matter.

Going through my clothes in the closet I thought about the last three months of my life. There was something about doing tedious work that made me think. With the exception of the house from my previous marriage, life had become good again. Major had kept his promise and allowed me time to find myself. He worked hard and pushed me to do the same. For now he was at peace with me just working Thursday through Saturday mornings. He played golf and was always waiting for me when I returned home. The only reason life wasn't perfect was because I had not become pregnant yet. Although I had become Mrs. Major Oswald Jasper and I loved every minute of it. The day my husband insisted on going to the courthouse was the happiest day of my life. It felt like it was the first day of a new life. A happy life and I was going to do everything in my power to keep it that way.

Day dreaming I grimaced in pain when I knocked down a wooden box from the top shelf in the huge closet. Groaning within I wanted to kick myself for creating more work for me to do. Lately I had been so fatigued all I wanted to do was sleep. I toyed with the fact that I could be pregnant, but had been so disappointed the previous month when I had believed the same thing and the test came back negative. I promised myself I would wait for at least another week before buying another test. Sitting on the plush teal carpet I started the task of picking up the numerous pieces of paper from the floor. Ready to see my husband I daydreamed even more as I cleaned my mess. Then it hit me like a swift kick in the gut. Hunger. Suddenly I was starving and eating was all I could think of doing. Wishing Major could join me for lunch I abandoned the papers in the floor and went to make a sandwich.

Not use to being at home so much, I turned on the television while eating my food. True to who I was I watched the news and court television until I was finished. Wishing I had more friends I went on social media trying to find some of my college friends, in particular Zoleen, but could not. The last thing I heard she had married and moved to Michigan. It was next to impossible finding someone and not having a correct last name. I wanted to apologize for what I put her through. We had fought about me returning to live with Finn after I left the hospital. She did not understand my actions. She never knew he had promised to kill her and my parents if I had contact with them. They thought my actions were deliberate, but I only wanted to protect them.

Growing bored I aimlessly wondered around the house until I remembered the mess I had left in the closet. Major would be home in a couple of hours and not completing a task he had assigned me was the quickest way to start an argument. Fight was the last thing in the world I wanted to do.

Again I sat on the floor picking up the papers that had fallen, seemingly from out of nowhere. This time I could not take my time. The clothes had to be done and the dinner must be finished and I was playing with papers. With the cleanup task almost completed, I was about to close the box when I saw a picture of my late husband. Swearing my eyes played tricks on me I closed the box anyway and returned it to the shelf and headed to the kitchen again. The attorney in me forced me to return to that box again. Opening it I thumbed through what looked like old receipts of some sort. The way I had tossed the box to the shelf because of my height, the contents had shifted. Relieved that it had only been a trick of the eye I concluded that I was just tired. The papers were just stuff that my husband, who never threw anything away had decided to keep. Until I saw a piece of paper with Finn Bardo written on it. Feeling sick I sat on the floor once more. Then, I saw the picture and was happy I had decided to sit down. Why would my late husband's full name, picture, and our home address be in a box in my new husband's home? Frantic, I searched the box for other items, wishing there would not be any. Piece by piece I combed through what appeared to be hundreds of receipts and money orders. When I found a random bank receipt for $10,000 dated December 11th, my heart sank. December 11th had been the day after I had slept all day. The day after my boss had given me time off. The day after Major set aside time for me to relax and enjoy the massage that I never took. The day after he spent time away from the hotel golfing and with some old friends. One day after the first time we made love.

Question after question, reason after reason as to the whys of the information that was before me. Was he capable of murder? Could I answer that question? I hardly knew him before we had rushed into marriage. Maybe it was all just a big mistake. If there was one thing I did not doubt, it was that Major Jasper loved me. I saw it in his eyes. Felt it in his touch. Heard it in his sleep. He loved me passionately, and made it clear he would do anything for me. Would he kill? Starting to perspire, my stomach suddenly felt sick and it was all I could do just to make it to the sink and fill it with my fear and anxiety. Repeatedly spewing my guts out, I felt worse and worse. Washing my face after I was finally empty, I put all of the papers back like I had found them and went straight to the bed. It was all I had the strength to do. When Major came home from work that was where he found me.

He took one look at me and knew something was wrong.

"What on earth is wrong with my sweet wife?"

I had known he would ask me that very same question. Lying did not go over well with him. Being one of the top attorneys in the state he was an expert at discerning people. He knew how to get information out of people. I would be no different. When I did not answer quickly enough he concluded immediately that I was hiding something. He was correct. He repeated his question again.

"Taylor darling, what is bothering you? Are you not feeling well?"

That was a question that I could answer truthfully and so having thought about it all afternoon I told him that truth and kept the box to myself.

"No my love. I have not felt that great lately."

"Maybe we should go to the doctor."

"Not necessary love. A little rest is all I need."

Eyeing me for too long I knew I was going to have to give him more because my story was still suspicious to him. Having worked so close with him for so long it came with the territory. We really knew each other's body chemistry better than most couples did. It was a part of our profession. Many times in the court room you were not able to verbally communicate so body language was the native tongue of an attorney.

"My wife being ill disturbs me. Get dressed. I have never known you to be ill and I do not like it."

"I am not sick love."

"Then what is wrong. Why are you sad?"

"I'm pregnant."

I saw the excitement in his eyes. The smile that anyone never really saw, except his wife on occasion, I wanted to pretend I had not seen the box.

"Pregnant, as in we are having a baby?"

"Yes, love. At least I believe so."

Joining me on the bed kissing me, hugging me and laughing uncontrollably I realized one thing. I really did love him. Somehow in the middle of the craziness of our lives I had fallen deeper in love with the wrong man, again.

"Are you happy?"

"It is what I have always wanted Taylor. To be a father. To have a woman who loved me for who I am."

Kissing me one last time he had a revelation. "Why aren't you happy about it Taylor?"

"I am."

"No, you are not. I can see it all over you."

"I am just a little scared is all, I promise. Maybe it is too soon. We have our whole lives together. I want to spend more time with it just being us."

"We can have a nanny if that is what you want my sweet beautiful wife."

"No. I want to raise our baby. Just you and I." Thinking about the fact that I could be wrong I hoped and prayed.

"Please don't get your hopes up too high yet. I still have to be certain."

"Then get up and let's go get a test. Just for the record, I know you would never have told me if you weren't positive."

"You know me too well."

"Remember that Taylor. But also remember I also want to do nothing except love you for the rest of my life. You were never supposed to be married to Finn Bardo. You were my wife all along."

The only reason my husband did not see the alarm on my face was because the doorbell suddenly rang. Guests were something we never had and both of us were curious. Following him to the door both of us were shocked to see two police officers standing on our doorsteps.

Swinging open the door wide, Major asked, "May I help you officer?"

"Sir we are looking for Taylor Jasper, formally known as Taylor Bardo."

Stepping out from behind my husband I curiously said, "I am Taylor Jasper officer. How may I help you?"

"Mrs. Jasper, would you step outside so we can speak with you for a moment?'

Major demands, "What's this all about?"

Obeying their request I assure my husband that it is fine and walk outside the door asking again, "How may I help you?"

"Mrs. Jasper, we are placing you under arrest for the murder of Finn Bardo. You have the right to remain silent…"

10

When the officer closed the jail cell behind me I grumbled to the floor. I had no one or nothing. My parents had renounced me as their child and I had no friends. My life was over and I knew it. I'd heard it in the finality of the bars slamming shut. I was pregnant and about to go to prison for a murder I was sure my new husband had committed. For that reason, I was sure he would not come and help me.

Hovered in the corner of the cold dirty floor I thought about how my parents had given up on me. I thought back to the day I realized that the people you love most hurt you the most. Wanting to reconcile with them and just see my daddy's beard and grey eyes got the better of me one day. Telling Major I was going to the store to shop for clothes, I only had intentions of driving to their home. So much had happened and all I wanted to do was see them. Taste my mother's hot chocolate and apple pie. When I arrived that day I was too afraid to go in so I parked across the street and watched the house to see if I could get a glimpse of them. My heart longed to see them and when the door finally opened I waited to see which one of them would come out. Only it was not either of them, but a stranger. A tall Caucasian man with a cane, followed by a woman that strongly resembled Mr. Ed and Ms. Piggy. Getting out of the car I ran across the street demanding to know where the people were that owned the house. When the lady, chewing gum at the speed of lightening said, "Hon, I don't know what to tell ya. This house belongs to me and my man here. We bought it fair and squares."

Not willing to believe that my parents would sell the only home they had lived in to total strangers, I demanded more information. Who could tell if there was any foul play taking place?

"I know the people who own this house and I know they would never sell it. They have a daughter and the house would belong to her if anything ever happened to them."

The woman answered again, "Like I says, the people of this house sold it to us. Nothing happened to them. Very nice people, Phil and Janice, they retired and decided to downsize and see the world is alls."

The elderly man, becoming impatient, yelled for her and she quickly said, "I have to go honey buns. The mister is calling for me."

Shocked I watched them drive away. Remembering how being an attorney had great privileges, I called in a few favors from one of the guys at the court house. It only took a couple of hours to confirm that what I had heard was indeed true. My parents were gone. No address. No goodbye. Gone. My family home had been sold six months after I married Finn Bardo.

My court appointed lawyer informed me that the circumstantial evidence that the state had against me would put me behind bars for a long time. He recommended that I confess and take the plea deal that they were willing to offer me. They were sure that the abuse that only Major knew about, and the very fact that I not only had a lover, but married him soon after Finn died was enough to convict me.

When I began to scream in the floor of the prison, the anguish of my soul could not be consoled. My husband had not been to see me; to bail me out. I was abandoned and all alone. My life was over and my baby would never have one. Not caring what the guards did to me, I screamed and yelled. I begged for God to help me; something that I had learned about so long ago in Vacation Bible School when my neighbors had taken me one summer. The God they said would hide you. The God they said would help you. The God the teacher said would keep your secrets and forgive your sins. I needed Him. I prayed He would not remember that I had ignored Him all my life.

Late into the night I cried until I had no more tears. Hearing footsteps I did not bother to look up. In the middle of the night the only people that visited jail cells were police officers with other criminals. When the bars never opened it made me wonder. Looking up I saw on the floor was a piece of paper folded in half. It puzzled me. Getting up from the floor I walked over and picked up the note. It read,

"Go to the secret place."

Matthew 6:6

But you, when you pray, go into your room, and when you have shut your door, pray to your Father who *is* in the secret *place;* and your Father who sees in secret will reward you openly.